GLASSES

FOR

WALLY

By Bryan Carrier

Published by Pen It! Publications, LLC in the U.S.A.

812-371-4128   www.penitpublications.com

ISBN: 978-1-952894-13-8

Illustrated by Jenni Wells

Dedication

I would like to dedicate, Glasses for Wally, to my mother, Janet Carrier. Together, we witnessed the bird that needed glasses.

And to my wife, Heather who I love very much, thank you for listening to all my crazy stories.

To the staff Pen It! Publishing for bringing Wally to life and my faithful readers for purchasing this book.

The animals in the forest gather at the river's edge to glimpse the poor macaw struggling to fly like his feathered friends.

"Hope he makes it this time,"
Harry the hippo bellows.

Wally flies wildly between branches.

He narrowly misses the giant jaws of a crocodile.

"Wally! Look out for that tree!" screams Sylvester the squirrel. Wally bounces off one branch then another spiraling out of control landing in a pile of leaves.

THUD!

"Are you hurt?" Sylvester asks.

"I'm afraid to fly. Everything is blurry."

His friends circle around him.
"I wear them!"

Benny the bookworm smiles
poking his black rimmed glasses
from behind a book.

"Glasses are a good idea," Ginny the giraffe sings, showing off her red glasses.

"I like my green glasses," Tory the turtle mumbles.

"Birds don't wear glasses," Wally explains to them.

"Neither do worms," Benny smiles.

"Neither do giraffes," Ginny smiles.

"Neither do turtles," Tory mumbles.

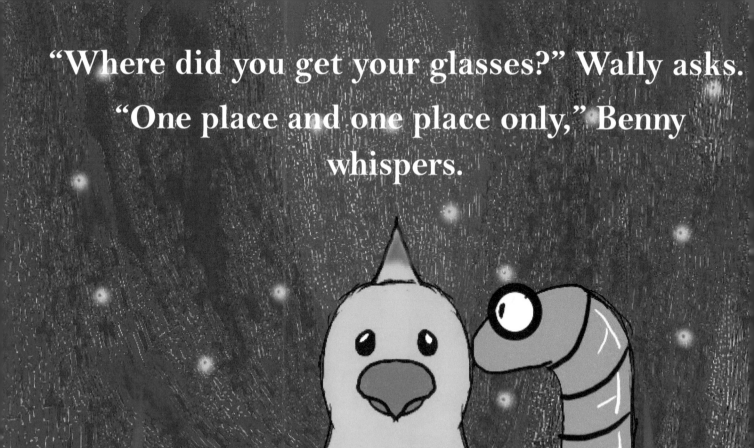

"Where did you get your glasses?" Wally asks.
"One place and one place only," Benny
whispers.

"If you dare," Ginny slurps between eating leaves.

"Where?" Wally asks.

"Maynard," Tory mumbles.

"The junkyard dog!" Sylvester squeals with fright.

"What about all those scary stories about him?" Wally asks.

"You want to fly, don't you?" Susie the snake hisses, coiling herself around a tree limb.

"More than anything," Wally chirps.

"I'm sure he's nice," Ginny the giraffe said.

"You never know if you don't go!" Casey the crocodile croons.

"You have to go!" Sylvester exclaims.

"How will I get there?" Wally asks.

"I'll take you," Tory mumbles.

"Don't be silly," Henry the hawk laughs. "Hop on!"

"But…" Wally shrieks.

"It's your best chance," Sylvester tells his friend.

Wally hops on Henry, disappearing from the woods.

Once in the city, Henry circles
the junkyard.

"There he is," Henry said.

He lands near Maynard who is
chained to a tire.

"Go ask him."

"But…"

"You can't judge a book by its cover," Henry explains to Wally.

As Wally approaches, Maynard opens one eye, "I heard you can't fly."

"I heard you were mean," says Wally.

"Let's help each other and become friends," Maynard said.

"I'd like that," Wally smiles.

"You get the key from the shed and the glasses," Maynard growls.

In the shed, Wally picks a key and glasses from a hook with his beak.

He drops the key to Maynard, as Henry ties the glasses to Wally's face.

Wally's tiny eyes blink behind the thick rims.

A man runs from the shed screaming, "Hey! Get back here!"

"Run!" Maynard growls.

Wally flies with Henry.

Maynard follows on the ground.

Maynard becomes friends with the animals in the forest.

"I can fly! I can fly!" Wally chirps, zooming around his friends.

"I'm free! I'm free!" Maynard barks.

Wally zooms in and out of the trees.

ZOOM! ZOOM! ZOOM!

As the sun sets, Wally becomes exhausted. He snuggles against Maynard, falling fast asleep.

The End

Author Bryan Carrier is a native of, Cleveland, Ohio who migrated to the warm sunny beaches of Clearwater, Florida in time to miss the snow flurries. He has an Associates degree in The Science of Graphic Arts Technology and Business. Bryan has worked in the graphic arts industry his entire career and is a Production Co-Ordinator in a busy printing facility. He enjoys writing children stories as well as screenplays. He has written pieces for the Vietnam Veteran's Memorial, Vietnam Women's Memorial, and Korean War Veteran's Memorial. He has also written a striking piece titled, Five More Minutes, for the Oklahoma City Bombing site. When he is not writing you can find him relaxing with his wife, Heather and their two dogs, Ruby and Bean.

CPSIA information can be obtained
at www.ICGtesting.com
Printed in the USA
LVHW070051201120
672011LV00002B/58